PRINCESS PULVERIZER

the dragon's tale

For Josie, a pup with plenty of her own tales to tell . . .

if only she could talk!—NK

PENGUIN WORKSHOP

An Imprint of Penguin Random House LLC, New York

Text copyright © 2019 by Nancy Krulik. Illustrations and logo copyright © 2019 by Penguin Random House LLC. All rights reserved. Published by Penguin Workshop, an imprint of Penguin Random House LLC, New York. PENGUIN and PENGUIN WORKSHOP are trademarks of Penguin Books Ltd, and the W colophon is a registered trademark of Penguin Random House LLC. Printed in the USA.

Visit us online at www.penguinrandomhouse.com.

Library of Congress Cataloging-in-Publication Data is available upon request.

ISBN 9781524791537 (pbk)   10 9 8 7 6 5 4 3 2 1
ISBN 9781524791544 (hc)   10 9 8 7 6 5 4 3 2 1

NANCY KRULIK

PRINCESS PULVERIZER

the dragon's tale

art by Justin Rodrigues
based on original character designs by
Ben Balistreri

CHAPTER 1

"Get your grilled cheese here!" Dribble
the dragon shouted as he held up plates of
perfectly melted mozzarella and tomato
sandwiches.

"Best grilled cheese in the whole world,"
Dribble's best friend, Lucas, added.

"Well, I don't know about *that*,"
Dribble's other pal, Princess Pulverizer,
argued.

Lucas and the dragon both glared at her.

"Well, I just mean, we haven't *been* all over the world," Princess Pulverizer said quickly, "so we don't actually know if Dribble makes the best grilled cheese."

"We don't actually know he *doesn't* make the best grilled cheese in the world, either," Lucas said.

"You have a point," Princess Pulverizer agreed. Then she shouted, "Get your grilled cheese here! It might be the best grilled cheese in the world . . . maybe."

Dribble called out to the people passing by, "Grilled mozzarella sandwiches for sale! Only one brass coin!"

That wasn't very expensive. And yet, not one person in the Beeten Wheeten village market came anywhere near the dragon's food stand. In fact, they all moved away as far as they could, and cowered nervously in the corners of the square.

"I don't understand why people are afraid of dragons," Dribble said sadly. "Most of us are very nice once you get to know us."

"You *are* nice," Lucas agreed. "People shouldn't blame all dragons just because a few bad ones burn down villages."

"Meanwhile, these sandwiches are getting cold," Dribble complained.

"I'll take care of that," Princess Pulverizer said. She grabbed a sandwich from Dribble's claws, smiled brightly at the people in the square, opened her mouth, and . . .

Promptly took a great, big bite!

"Hey!" Dribble exclaimed. "I thought you were going to *sell* that sandwich."

"I never said that," Princess Pulverizer

replied. "I said I'd take care of it." She took another big bite of the sandwich. Gooey mozzarella cheese oozed out all over her face. She used her sleeve to wipe it off, then took another bite. "Delicious!" she exclaimed as she chewed with her mouth open.

Lucas looked at her and shook his head. "What would your teacher at the Royal School of Ladylike Manners say?"

Princess Pulverizer knew exactly what Lady Frump would say. "'I don't know what I'm going to do with you!'" Princess

Pulverizer replied, doing her best imitation of her teacher—complete with her hands in the air and her eyes rolling wildly.

Lucas burst out laughing.

Dribble didn't. "I'm glad you two think this is so funny," he said sadly. "How can I become a world-famous chef if no one will eat my sandwiches? I'm never going to make my dream come true."

Huge purple dragon tears slid down Dribble's face and onto the ground, leaving a small purple puddle by his feet.

"We have to do something for him," Lucas whispered to Princess Pulverizer.

"Yes," Princess Pulverizer agreed. "We have to cheer him up *right away*. It's not good for him to be this sad."

Lucas looked at her, amazed.

"What?" Princess Pulverizer demanded.

"It's just that . . . well . . . I mean, I've never seen you care about how other people feel before," Lucas explained. "You're usually more concerned about how *you* feel."

Princess Pulverizer put her hand to her heart. "Lucas! How can you say such a thing? I'm going to be a knight. And knights care very much about other people's feelings."

"I'm sorry," Lucas apologized. "I didn't mean to insult you."

"That's okay." It wasn't hard for Princess Pulverizer to forgive him. Especially because Lucas wasn't completely wrong. The princess didn't *only* care about Dribble's feelings. She also cared about how Dribble's sadness was going to affect *her*.

Princess Pulverizer needed Dribble's help if she was ever going to be allowed to go to Knight School. And that was Princess Pulverizer's greatest dream. She wanted it more than anything. Maybe even more than Dribble wanted to be a chef.

But just as Dribble was going to have to overcome obstacles if he was going to open his own restaurant, Princess Pulverizer was going to have to go through a lot to make her dream come true.

And it was all her father's idea!

When Princess Pulverizer had asked King Alexander if she could go to Knight School, he'd flat out told her no. But she hadn't given up. And eventually she was able to convince her father to let her go to Knight School. Which she had totally expected, seeing as Princess Pulverizer usually got her way.

Only the king wasn't going to let her go right away.

Now that was *not* expected.

The king told Princess Pulverizer that she had to go on a Quest of Kindness and complete eight good deeds. It was the only way she was ever going to learn how not to be selfish, spoiled, and snobby.

Because knights are *never* selfish, spoiled, and snobby.

Princess Pulverizer had been on her Quest of Kindness for what seemed like a very long time now. And with the help of her new friends, Lucas and Dribble, she'd done *a lot* of good deeds.

Like overcoming an ogre.

Taking on a terrible troll.

And outfencing a fearful foe.

Along the way, the princess had learned a lot about being brave. And thinking of others. And being more patient.

She'd also learned to be part of a team. She could never have done those good deeds without the help of Dribble and Lucas.

Which was why she needed Dribble to stop crying. The princess had only completed five good deeds so far. She still had three more to go, and she couldn't do them without the dragon's help. But he was in no state to help her right then.

Princess Pulverizer wished she knew when Dribble might stop crying and they could continue their Quest of Kindness. Unfortunately, there was no way she could predict the future.

Or was there?

Quickly, Princess Pulverizer reached into her knapsack and pulled out a hand mirror. It had been a gift from Anna, the good witch of Starats.

The mirror was beautiful, magical, and—at the moment—extremely helpful.

Because this mirror could predict the future.

"I think you wiped off all the mozzarella grease," Lucas said as he watched the princess peer into the mirror.

"I'm not looking for grease," Princess
Pulverizer said. "I'm looking to see if this
magic mirror can predict exactly where
Dribble will be when he stops crying."

"What good will that do?" Lucas asked.

"Once we know where he will be when he becomes happy again, we can take him there and wait for him to start smiling," the princess explained.

Dribble let out a loud sob. Three more tears fell to the ground. The purple puddles were getting deeper.

"Hurry," Lucas urged the princess.

Princess Pulverizer looked into the magic mirror. The picture was cloudy—as if there was a film of dirt over its surface. Little by little, it began to clear.

"Here it comes," Princess Pulverizer said happily. "Any minute now we will know . . . *uh-oh*."

"What do you mean, *uh-oh*?" Lucas asked nervously.

"The mirror isn't showing Dribble," Princess Pulverizer said. "It's showing *you*."

"Me? In the future?" Lucas asked, surprised.

Princess Pulverizer turned the mirror around. "See?"

Lucas stared at his image in the magic mirror. In it, his mouth was wide open. His arms were spread out like wings. And behind him were clouds and treetops.

"That's me all right," Lucas agreed nervously. *And I'm flying!"*

CHAPTER 2

The very idea of his best buddy floating in midair was enough to stop Dribble from crying.

"Flying?" the dragon repeated. "How? Even *I* can't fly. And I have wings."

"*Baby* wings," Princess Pulverizer reminded him. "When your grown-up wings grow in, you'll fly just fine."

"But I don't have any wings at all," Lucas said. "So how can I fly?"

"Who knows?" Princess Pulverizer said. "We'll have to wait until you actually start flying to find out."

"That's *not* happening," Lucas told his friends. "I'm leaving Beeten Wheeten. I can't *fly* here if I'm *not* here."

"That's just silly," Princess Pulverizer told him.

"You mean because it's impossible for a person to fly?" Dribble asked her.

"No, because the mirror didn't necessarily show Lucas flying in Beeten

Wheeten. It didn't show *where* or *when* Lucas was flying at all," Princess Pulverizer said. "If we leave here, he might take flight in the very next town."

"That's not exactly reassuring," Lucas said nervously.

"Come on," Princess Pulverizer urged. "I know just the thing to take both your minds off your troubles."

Lucas looked at Dribble. "I don't think we're going to like this," he said.

"We need to look for someone with really *big* problems, who needs our help," Princess Pulverizer continued. "Maybe there's a monster in this town that needs defeating. Like a serpent-headed hydra. Or a giant man-eating spider. Or a—"

"I told you we weren't going to like this," Lucas whispered to Dribble.

"I doubt we will run into any creatures like those," Dribble assured his pal. "Besides, there's no point in staying here in the market," he added sadly. "Why not walk around for a bit?"

As Princess Pulverizer and her pals wandered around Beeten Wheeten, the princess found herself getting quite discouraged. It didn't seem like anyone had any troubles at all.

Which was *very* troubling to the princess. Now Dribble and Lucas weren't the only ones who were unhappy. She needed some cheering up as well.

This time, it was Lucas who found just the thing. "Hey, look!" he exclaimed. "There's a juggling show. Let's go watch."

Princess Pulverizer shrugged. They might as well sit and rest their feet. "Okay," she said. "But just for a little while."

The three friends took seats on a crowded bench. Well, the bench *started out* crowded, anyway. The minute the people sitting there spotted Dribble, they leaped up and ran off.

Dribble looked like he might start crying all over again.

"Never mind," Lucas told him gently. "Now there's more room for us."

A woman walked onto the small, makeshift wooden stage and smiled at the audience—revealing that she was missing two teeth. "And now The Amazing Ralf will juggle fire!" she announced.

A man in a top hat wandered onto the stage. "Thank you, Bertha," The Amazing Ralf said as he held up three wooden torches. "Light these, please."

Bertha pulled pieces of flint and steel from her pocket and banged them together until a small spark appeared. Quickly, she used cloth as kindling to make a flame and lit the ends of the torches.

"Here we go!" The Amazing Ralf shouted excitedly as he began to juggle.

He tossed one torch in the air. And caught it.

He tossed the second torch in the air. And caught it.

He tossed the third torch in the air. And . . . *THUD!* The flaming piece of wood hit the ground with a shower of sparks. Within seconds the stage caught fire.

"Fire!" someone in the crowd yelled. "Run!"

"No need to leave," The Amazing Ralf said calmly. "My lovely wife Bertha's got it all under control."

Princess Pulverizer watched as the juggler's assistant poured a huge bucket of water over the flames.

"We always have water handy, just in case we need it," The Amazing Ralf said.

"We pretty much *always* need it," Bertha muttered as she grabbed a mop and started cleaning up the wet, sooty mess.

The crowd began to boo. Some folks threw wilted lettuce and rotting tomatoes at the stage.

"Great!" The Amazing Ralf cheered. "These will make a delicious stew."

The audience booed louder. Someone threw a shoe.

The Amazing Ralf picked it up. "Just my size," he said. "Now I have a pair. Although I think they are both for my right foot."

"The Amazing Ralf isn't very amazing," Princess Pulverizer complained.

"And now for my greatest trick," Ralf announced. "I will need some assistance from a member of the audience." He wandered into the crowd, searching for just the right helper. He stopped when he reached the bench where Princess Pulverizer, Dribble, and Lucas were sitting.

"You will do just fine," Ralf said, pointing directly at Lucas.

"M-m-me?" Lucas stammered. "No way."

"Oh go on," Princess Pulverizer urged. "What's the worst that can happen?"

"Why don't *you* go then?" Lucas asked.

"He's not asking me," Princess Pulverizer replied. "Besides, I thought you were trying hard not to be so lily-livered."

That last argument was enough to convince Lucas to stand and follow the juggler up onto the stage. The crowd began to cheer.

Ralf grabbed Lucas by the waist and hoisted him in the air. "I will now juggle this young man!" he announced.

"You're going to juggle *who*?" Lucas asked nervously.

"Juggle *you*," Ralf told him. "And this bottle. And a red rubber ball. There's nothing to worry about. I've tried this trick a million times."

"Somehow that doesn't make me feel any better," Lucas replied.

"Here we go!" Ralf tossed the ball in the air and caught it.

Then he tossed the bottle in the air and caught it.

Then he tossed both, along with Lucas, in the air and . . . caught him in his arms.

The crowd cheered.

"See?" Ralf told Lucas. "No problem. This time I will toss you higher."

"No!" Lucas cried out. "That was high enough."

But Ralf wasn't listening. He threw Lucas up in the air.

"AAAHHHH!" Lucas shouted. He spread his arms wide and looked exactly as he had in the magic mirror.

That's when the princess remembered the warning Anna the good witch had given her: The future she saw in the mirror might not turn out to be exactly as she thought it would be.

Lucas wasn't flying. He had just been juggled.

Clink. Clank. CLUNK.

And then he *wasn't* in the air anymore.

Ralf missed catching Lucas as he plummeted back down to the ground. The small knight-in-training landed on his rear end. The crowd laughed. Lucas turned bright red. "Can we go NOW?" he demanded as he climbed off the stage and stormed over to where Princess Pulverizer and Dribble were sitting.

"Definitely," Princess Pulverizer agreed. "Ralf is an awful juggler."

"You stink," one guy called out to Ralf, throwing a tomato at his head.

"It wasn't my fault. I know how to juggle," Ralf insisted. "It was that kid. He didn't know how to *be* juggled."

"It wasn't Lucas's fault!" Princess Pulverizer said, defending her friend.

"Don't blame my little buddy," Dribble added, leaping to his feet.

"AAAAHHHHH! Dragon!" someone shouted.

The audience members ran off in fear.

"You kids are a pain in my neck," Ralf told Dribble, Lucas, and Princess Pulverizer as he hopped off the stage. He pointed to Lucas. "First *you* ruin my show. Then this dragon scares off the audience before I can pass the hat and get some coins."

The princess rolled her eyes. The only thing Ralf would have gotten in that hat were a few rotted carrots the audience

hadn't had the chance to throw.

"Come on, you guys," she said. "Let's get away from this clown."

"I'm not a clown! I'm a juggler!" Ralf insisted angrily.

"You could have fooled me," Princess Pulverizer replied as she walked away.

"You three are going to be sorry," Ralf warned. "Mark my words."

CHAPTER 3

"Can we leave Beeten Wheeten now?"
Lucas asked as the three friends sat in the
forest that evening. "This village hasn't
been lucky for us. Dribble's pop-up grilled
cheese shop was no success, and—"

"That wasn't my fault," Dribble interrupted.

"I know," Lucas agreed. "And it wasn't my fault I got dropped by a lousy juggler."

Princess Pulverizer understood what Lucas was saying. But she wasn't ready to give up on finding a good deed to do in Beeten Wheeten. Every town had its problems, and she was determined to find the trouble here. Still, it wasn't going to be easy getting her friends to stay.

"I'm sorry, buddy," Dribble said. "I shouldn't have let you be bullied into going onstage." The dragon held a sandwich close to his mouth and let out a small flame. "Here," he told Lucas. "It's your favorite. Goat cheese and raspberry jam."

"Thanks," Lucas said, taking a big bite.

"Delicious, too!" he added.

Just then, Princess Pulverizer heard people talking.

"Hey, anybody smell grilled cheese?"

"Yeah, I do. And it's making me hungry."

The voices were coming from someone at the edge of the woods, hidden from the princess and her pals by a grove of thick trees. But their words were clear as day.

Dribble made a face. "As long as they don't know the grilled cheese sandwiches are made by a *dragon*, they want them just fine."

That was it! Princess Pulverizer knew exactly how to get her friends to stay—

at least for a day or two while she looked
for a good deed to do.

"Dribble, you've just given me a great
idea!" she declared.

"Three more cheddar and tomato on
rye, Dribble," Princess Pulverizer said
as she ran back into the forest the next
afternoon. "Those are a huge hit."

"You have to wait," Lucas told her.
"He's busy making my jalapeño pepper
cheese nachos."

"I can't believe how many customers we have," Princess Pulverizer said.

"This was a great idea," Lucas complimented her.

"One of my best," Princess Pulverizer agreed proudly.

"Boastful much?" Dribble asked her.

"Don't complain," said the princess. "You're selling a lot of grilled cheese. Who cares if the customers don't know it's a dragon that's making them?"

"I do," Dribble said. "You can't be a famous chef if no one knows you're a chef."

"We will tell them—eventually," Princess Pulverizer assured him. "But for now, this is a good way to sell your sandwiches. It's the first step toward making you famous."

"I guess you're right." Dribble still sounded disappointed.

"Of course I'm right," Princess Pulverizer said. "You stay hidden behind the trees and cook. Lucas and I go into that field and serve. Everybody wins."

Princess Pulverizer bit her lip. She'd said too much. She didn't want Lucas or Dribble to ask her how *she* would be winning. After all, she didn't want to tell them that she was selfishly searching for an evildoer among the customers.

Because selfishness wasn't knightly.

But hard work *was*. And waitressing was definitely hard. Her feet were killing her.

To make matters worse, Princess Pulverizer had been serving sandwiches for hours and so far no one had shown the slightest sign of cruelty. Or evil. Or danger. There wasn't even anyone being impolite. The princess had never heard so many people say *please*, *thank you*, or *excuse me* in her life.

Dribble breathed a tiny flame onto the edges of a pile of cheese-covered corn chips. "These nachos are done," he told Lucas. "Take them to your customers."

As Lucas carried out the dish of nachos, Dribble began grilling three sandwiches at the same time.

"Impressive," Princess Pulverizer
complimented him.

"You're a really great friend," Dribble thanked her. "It was so kind of you to set all this up just for me."

The princess felt a twinge of guilt.

"These sandwiches are ready," Dribble said, handing her three plates.

Princess Pulverizer balanced the plates on her arm and walked into the field where the customers were sitting.

"Here you go," she said, placing the plates on the ground in front of a picnicking family of three.

"Thank you," the father said.

"Thank you," the mother said.

"Thank you," the little girl added.

Princess Pulverizer sighed. All this politeness was really getting to her.

Just then, Princess Pulverizer heard someone yelling behind her. *I ordered baked brie on a roll!*"

Yes! Finally someone was acting mean. It was time for a true act of kindness.

"I'm sorry," Lucas apologized to the angry man nervously. "I can take it back and get you your sandwich."

Princess Pulverizer braced herself for an argument. She was ready to leap in and help.

"I guess that's *nacho* cheese sandwich, Maxwell," the woman sitting beside him said with a laugh.

Princess Pulverizer rolled her eyes.

"Nope," Maxwell replied. He took a chip from the plate and shoved it in his mouth. "But they're delicious. Please, bring us some more nachos, young man. And give my compliments to the chef."

Princess Pulverizer unclenched her fist. There would be no argument happening here. Which was very disappointing.

"What do you think you're doing?"

Princess Pulverizer was shocked out of her disappointment by a familiar voice. She turned around to see Ralf and Bertha standing right behind her.

"We're serving grilled cheese," Princess Pulverizer told him. "It's a bit of a wait if you don't have a reservation. But we can fit you in after about a half an hour."

"No, thanks," Ralf told her. "I don't

have any money. Your big dragon buddy
scared away my whole audience before I
could pass the hat around."

"Oh please," Princess Pulverizer
groaned. "You weren't getting any money

for that act. Don't blame Dribble."

"We need every penny we can get," Bertha complained. "I can't make much from the garbage that people throw at Ralf when he messes up. Most of it is too rotten."

"I do *not* mess up," Ralf insisted. He turned to Princess Pulverizer. "But you know what *is* a mess? You. You have cheese hanging from your hair and stains on your clothes. I'm going to report you to the authorities and have this restaurant closed down. It's not safe for people to eat in such filth."

Princess Pulverizer laughed. "You make dinner out of food scraps. Who are you to say what's safe to eat?"

Ralf glared angrily at the princess. "I'm going to get rid of your restaurant," he assured her. "Just you wait and see."

"I don't have time to wait for you," Princess Pulverizer told Ralf. "I have *paying* customers to wait on."

With that she turned and walked toward the woods where Dribble was making more sandwiches.

But before she reached him, Princess Pulverizer touched her hair. Sure enough, she could feel some gooey cheese stuck in there. Princess Pulverizer wasn't completely certain that the restaurant couldn't be shut down for something like that, but why take any chances?

The princess reached into her knapsack and pulled out her hand mirror so she could pull the cheese from her hair. But when she looked in the mirror, she didn't see her reflection at all. Instead, the mirror showed an old red barn surrounded by flames. Which was awful.

But the fire wasn't the worst part.

What made the mirror's prediction even worse was the fact that Dribble was standing right next to the burning barn. *And he had smoke coming from his snout!*

The princess shoved the mirror back into her knapsack before anyone else could catch a glimpse of what she had just seen.

The magic mirror's prediction of the future had to be wrong. Her friend could never ever do such a thing. *Could he?*

CHAPTER 4

"Boy am I thirsty!" Dribble said after the customers had left. "Breathing fire all day is exhausting."

"So is serving food all day," Lucas said. "I can't wait to crawl into a bed of nice soft pine needles."

Princess Pulverizer was also tired and thirsty. But she wasn't really thinking about it at the moment. She was too busy watching Dribble for any signs that he was becoming the kind of evil dragon who burned down buildings.

But he still seemed like good old Dribble. In fact, at the moment, he was letting Lucas ride on his tail as they went down to the river for a cold drink.

There was no way Dribble could be guilty of burning down any barn. The mirror had to be wrong.

"This isn't exactly the cleanest river I've ever seen," Lucas said as he climbed down from his perch on Dribble's tail.

A big chicken bone and some moldy pieces of bread floated by.

"I don't care," Dribble said. "I'm thirsty. And this is water." He bent his neck low, reached his snout into the river, and started slurping. "Very, very cold water."

Slurp. Slurp. Slurp.

"You're going to be spending a lot of time going to the bathroom tonight,"

Princess Pulverizer warned Dribble.

"I guess it couldn't hurt to take a sip," Lucas said. "I'll just try to drink around that trash."

He walked over and bent down to take a sip. "The water tastes pretty good," he called. "And it's really cold. I—"

BONK.

"Whoa!" Lucas shouted. "I just got hit with an old shoe. What's that doing floating in a river?"

Princess Pulverizer had no idea. But no way was she going to take a drink from any river that had shoes swimming in it along with the fish.

"I think I'll just have fruit juice in the morning," Princess Pulverizer said. "Let's go. I need sleep. And we still have to gather enough pine needles to build beds."

"One minute," Dribble called back to her between slurps. "Just a few more sips."

Slurp. Slurp. Sl—

"AAAHHH! There's a dragon drinking from our river!" a woman shouted as she neared the water's edge.

"Get out," her friend added. "We don't let dragons drink here."

Dribble stared at the two women. Big purple tears formed in his eyes.

"Don't let them bother you," Lucas
said, patting his pal on the back. "We were
getting ready to leave anyway."

"Sometimes humans can be very, very
mean," Dribble grumbled.

"I had no idea feet could hurt this badly,"
Princess Pulverizer complained as she
finally lay down on a bed of pine needles
a while later. She shut her eyes and tried

not to think about the ginormous blister forming on her little toe.

"Maybe we need to hire a few extra waiters to help serve our customers from now on," Dribble suggested.

Princess Pulverizer's eyes popped open wide. *From now on?* Did Dribble think his restaurant was going to be a permanent thing in Beeten Wheeten?

Princess Pulverizer hadn't minded lifting Dribble's spirits with one day of selling his sandwiches. But that was it. She still had three more good deeds to go on her quest. And there clearly were no deeds needing to be done here.

Besides, the princess couldn't get that image of Dribble next to the burning barn out of her head. The sooner she got him out of Beeten Wheeten, the better.

But she was way too tired to argue with Dribble now. There would be time for that in the morn . . .

Zzzz. Zzzzzzzzzz. ZZZZZZZZZZZ.

"What was that?" Princess Pulverizer shot up in bed and tried to see in the darkness.

There was nothing there.

She'd probably just snored herself awake. Again. Even she had to admit that she snored pretty loudly.

Crack . . . Snap . . . CRASH!

That was not her snoring. It couldn't be. The princess wasn't asleep.

"Hey. Did you guys hear that?" she whispered to Dribble and Lucas.

"I think I heard something," Lucas

replied in a sleepy voice.

"How about you, Dribble?" Princess
Pulverizer asked.

The dragon didn't answer.

The princess looked over at the dragon's
bed. It was empty—except for the heavy
golden mace he carried as the group
traveled.

"Dribble?" Princess Pulverizer called loudly. "Where are you?"

There was still no answer.

"Hey, do you smell smoke?" Lucas asked Princess Pulverizer. "I think it's coming from the direction of that farm we passed earlier."

Princess Pulverizer gulped. Farm? *Uh-oh.* Farms usually had wooden barns.

Which could go up in flames.

Which could have been started by a dragon.

A dragon who was suddenly mysteriously missing.

CHAPTER 5

"Run faster!" Princess Pulverizer
ordered as they ran toward the smoke.
"There could be people
who need saving."

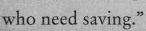

"I'm moving as fast as I can," Lucas answered, panting. "It's hard to run while carrying this heavy mace. That's usually Dribble's job. Where is he, anyway?"

Princess Pulverizer didn't answer. She was trying not to think about where Dribble might be. *Or what he might have done.*

"You could have left the mace at our campsite," the princess told Lucas.

"I was worried someone might be hurt," Lucas said. "The magic in this mace might be able to cure someone's injuries."

Princess Pulverizer certainly hoped no one had been hurt. Because if Dribble had started a fire, burning a barn was one thing. But hurting someone was far worse.

No. It couldn't have been Dribble.

The princess tried imagining all the

other possible creatures that could have caused a terrible fire to break out. Creatures that needed to be stopped by Princess Pulverizer!

Perhaps the fire had been set by a yelping yeti.

Or a massive, man-eating moth.

Or a . . . *dragon.*

As she reached the farm, the princess saw Dribble standing by a burning barn with smoke coming from his snout.

Just as he had appeared in the mirror.

A crowd had gathered around the farmer and his wife, who were looking at the fire.

"That dragon burned down my barn!" the farmer shouted.

The farmer was dressed in bright red footie pajamas and wore a straw hat.

Princess Pulverizer would have burst
out laughing at the sight of him, had the
situation not been so serious.

"Did you actually see Dribble set the
fire?" Lucas demanded.

Princess Pulverizer was impressed.
Lucas sounded so brave trying to defend
his friend.

"I didn't actually *see* him," the farmer

replied. "But that's what dragons do, isn't it? They burn towns, villages—and *barns*."

"We need a knight!" his wife added. "Someone who will slay this dragon!"

"Slay the dragon! Slay the dragon!" the crowd began to chant.

"You can't slay Dribble," Lucas argued. "You can't prove he set that fire."

Princess Pulverizer placed her hand on the sword at her side. But she couldn't bring herself to draw it. Sure, slaying a dragon who set a barn on fire and endangered people's lives would be a good deed. But there was no way she could slay *this* dragon.

Dribble was good. And kind. There was no way he'd set a barn on fire.

At least Princess Pulverizer didn't *think* he would.

"He's running away!" the farmer shouted. "Somebody grab that dragon."

"Not me," one man cried.

"I'm not messing with any dragon," another man added.

No one from Beeten Wheeten was willing to try to stop Dribble from running off.

"Run, Dribble!" Lucas shouted. "Get away from here!"

Lucas might have been pleased that Dribble was getting away, but Princess Pulverizer wasn't. Running off made Dribble look guiltier than he had before.

As she watched Dribble disappear into the woods, Princess Pulverizer spotted someone standing far from the crowd. It was Ralf. And he was smiling like this was the happiest night of his life.

As the princess caught his eye, Ralf strolled over. "It's a shame your friend was run out of town just as your little restaurant was getting popular," he said.

Ralf's smug smile made Princess Pulverizer very angry. But she wasn't going to let him know that. Knights were supposed to remain calm and reasonable. At least that's how her father's royal knights seemed to be. So she calmly told Ralf, "Dribble will be back once I prove he didn't burn down the barn."

"If you *can* prove it," Ralf said.

"What's that supposed to mean?" Princess Pulverizer demanded.

"Just that it's possible he did burn it down," Ralf replied. "And even if he didn't, how do you plan to prove it?"

Hmmm . . . that was a tough one.

Princess Pulverizer rested her hands on her hips for a minute and thought.

As Princess Pulverizer's fingers brushed against her sword, her face brightened. "I'll just ask Dribble if he set the barn on fire. And when he denies it, I'll have all the proof I need."

"Anyone who is capable of burning down a barn is capable of lying," Ralf pointed out.

Princess Pulverizer pulled out her sword. "This is a truth-telling sword. If someone is lying, it will wiggle. But if he's telling the truth, it will lie still. This sword will clear Dribble's name."

Ralf laughed. "A truth-telling sword. Who's going to believe that? You're a stranger. And you're friendly with a *dragon*. That doesn't exactly make you someone folks will trust."

Ralf had a point. Still, on the other hand . . .

"Who's to say *you* didn't burn down the barn?" Princess Pulverizer asked Ralf. "You almost started a fire at your own show yesterday. You're just as much a possible suspect as Dribble."

"What reason would I have to burn a barn?" Ralf asked her.

"I don't know," Princess Pulverizer admitted. "Maybe you were practicing juggling fire and you missed."

"Impossible," Ralf replied. "I don't practice."

After seeing his rotten show, Princess Pulverizer believed that. Still, who knew what evil Ralf was capable of?

"If your friend *is* innocent, I have a way

for you to prove it," Ralf continued.

"Why should I trust you?" the princess asked. "You hate Dribble."

"*Hate* is such a strong word," Ralf replied. "Let's just be friends, okay?" He held out his hand. The princess shook it cautiously.

"So how exactly can I prove Dribble's innocence?" she asked Ralf.

"Meet me in the meadow at dawn," Ralf replied mysteriously. "I'll fill you in on the details then."

CHAPTER 6

"I don't trust Ralf," Lucas said nervously as he followed Princess Pulverizer toward the meadow right before dawn.

"That's just because he dropped you in the middle of his show," Princess Pulverizer replied.

"And because he warned us that we were going to be sorry after his audience walked out," Lucas reminded her. "I can't help thinking we're heading into a trap."

Princess Pulverizer was thinking the same thing. But what else could she do? She had to prove Dribble was innocent. And Ralf was the only person in town who had said he could do that. It was a chance they were going to have to take.

"Ah, you're here," Ralf greeted Princess Pulverizer and Lucas as they approached.

"Now tell us how we can clear Dribble's name so we can *leave*," Lucas said.

Ralf shot him an angry look.

"*Please,*" Lucas added nervously.

Ralf gave them a creepy grin. "The solution to your problem is in here." The juggler reached into his pocket and pulled out a small book. The title on the cover read *Unicorns from A to Z.*

The princess was confused. "What do unicorns have to do with Dribble?"

"It's right here on page 37. *Unicorns have the unique ability to spot a liar,*" Ralf read. "*If a unicorn senses someone is telling a lie, he will poke him with his horn.* So if your friend Dribble says he didn't burn down the barn, and he's telling the truth, the unicorn will let him be. But if he's lying, the unicorn will poke him with his horn. All we have to do is get Dribble and a unicorn together in the village and let everyone hear what Dribble has to say."

"How is that any different than my

truth-telling sword?" the princess asked.

"No one in Beeten Wheeten has heard of a truth-telling sword," Ralf reminded her. "*Everyone* has heard of unicorns. Plus, this is in a book. So it must be true."

"Where are we supposed to find a unicorn?" Lucas pointed out. "No one has ever seen a real one before."

Ralf smiled so wide, Princess Pulverizer could see where his teeth were missing way in the back. "I've seen one," he said. "Right here in this meadow."

Princess Pulverizer's eyes opened wide. "You saw a real live unicorn?"

"Of course," Ralf replied. "Is there any other kind?"

Lucas gave Ralf a suspicious look. "Even if you actually did see a unicorn, how are we going to get it to help us?"

"That's where she comes in," Ralf explained, pointing at Princess Pulverizer. "Unicorns are timid around almost everyone. But they will come and lay their heads in the laps of kind girls. You, young lady, are going to be that girl."

Lucas pulled Princess Pulverizer aside.

"Um . . . excuse us," the princess said quickly to Ralf. Then she turned to Lucas. "What?" she demanded.

"I don't like this," Lucas whispered. "Why would Ralf want to help us? What's in it for him?"

Princess Pulverizer should have been wondering the same thing. But the chance to meet a real unicorn was too tempting.

"Okay," she said, walking back over to Ralf. "What do I do?"

"Just sit here in the meadow," Ralf

replied. "The unicorn will come to you."

"That's all?" the princess asked.

"That's all," Ralf repeated. He turned to Lucas. "You and I have to hide in the woods. Unicorns are shy. They don't like to be around a lot of people."

"I'm not leaving her alone," Lucas said.

"It's okay," the princess assured him.

"See?" Ralf said. "She's fine. Besides, you want to help Dribble, don't you?"

Lucas scrunched up his face. "Okay," he finally agreed. "But I'm warning you. I'm staying right at the edge of the woods so I can keep an eye on things."

Princess Pulverizer was impressed. Lucas was sounding less and less lily-livered every day. But it wasn't necessary. The princess didn't need anyone looking out for her.

"Fine," Ralf told Lucas. "You go to that corner, and I'll go on the other side. That way we can *both* keep an eye on things."

As Ralf and Lucas took to their separate corners in the woods, Princess Pulverizer sat on the damp grass and waited.

She twisted her tongue around in her mouth.

She twirled her hair with her fingers.

And wiggled her toes inside her boots.

She was not very good at waiting.

Just as Princess Pulverizer was about to give up, she saw it. *The unicorn.* He looked like a cross between a white horse and a soft-furred goat. And in the center of his head was a single white horn.

A unicorn! An actual unicorn!

The princess didn't move. She barely breathed. She didn't want to do anything that might scare him away.

The unicorn cautiously edged closer and closer to Princess Pulverizer. And then, just as Ralf had predicted, the gentle creature laid its head right in her lap.

Princess Pulverizer reached down and gently petted his head.

WHOOOSH! Suddenly a giant lasso whirred above the princess.

The unicorn looked up, frightened. And as he lifted his head, the lasso swung down over him, catching around his neck.

"Gotcha!" Ralf shouted out.

"What are you doing?" Princess Pulverizer demanded.

Ralf laughed. "I'm capturing a unicorn. And I'm going to charge people a pretty penny to see him. This horse with a horn is going to make me rich. And no one will have money for your grilled cheese sandwiches anymore. I told you I'd get rid of your restaurant!"

"But you . . . you . . ." The princess was so angry, she couldn't speak.

"Oh come on. You didn't think I actually wanted to help you, did you?"

Ralf asked with a laugh. He dragged the unicorn closer to the woods, where he had a cage on wheels hidden in the trees, waiting. Then he forced the unicorn into the cage and slammed the door shut.

"We're out of here," Ralf said as he began to wheel the cage away. "And I think it's time for you and your little friend over there to be on your way." He pointed to Lucas, who was now running as quickly as he could toward the meadow.

As Ralf rolled the cage away, Princess Pulverizer caught a glimpse of the unicorn. The magnificent creature was huddled in the corner, shaking with fear.

It hurt the princess terribly to think she had played a part in his capture.

"I knew Ralf was up to no good," Lucas said as he reached the princess. "What are we going to do now?"

"I'll tell you what we're *not* going to do," Princess Pulverizer replied. "We're *not* leaving Beeten Wheeten. We're going to free that unicorn. And we're going to find out who really set the barn on fire."

"That's a lot to do," Lucas said.

"Yup," Princess Pulverizer replied. "So we'd better get started."

CHAPTER 7

"Ralf was right about one thing," Lucas said later that day as he and the princess walked past a long line near the juggler's stage. "People will pay to see a real unicorn."

Princess Pulverizer didn't—*couldn't*—answer. The lump in her throat was too big. Just the thought of that poor unicorn being stuck in a cage on display made her want to cry. And knights never cried.

At least she didn't *think* they did.

"What's *that* long line for?" Lucas asked her, pointing to a second, even longer line.

A wave of fear came over the princess. *What other helpless creature might Ralf have captured?*

"What is this line for?" she asked a woman standing near the end.

"The public bathroom," the woman answered. "And these people are all taking too long. My stomach is killing me."

"You're not the only one," the man in front of her chimed in. "We all have bellyaches today. It's been going on for a couple of weeks actually."

"But it seems a lot worse lately," the woman added. "Some sort of flu, I fear."

Princess Pulverizer jumped back. If there was a stomach bug going around, she certainly didn't want to catch it.

"Come on, Lucas," she said. "We can't wait around here. We have to find Dribble."

"Can we wait a minute?" Lucas asked. "My stomach's not feeling so great, either."

"We'll find you another bathroom somewhere," Princess Pulverizer assured him. "Right now, we have work to do."

"What's that stink?" Lucas wondered as he and Princess Pulverizer walked toward the woods. "It smells like old socks."

"It is," the princess agreed. "There's a pair floating in the river over there."

"Oh yeah," Lucas said. "Over by that half-eaten turkey drumstick. Hey, are those underpants floating by the rocks?"

"Come on, Lucas," Princess Pulverizer urged. "We don't have time to watch the river flow. We have to find Dribble."

"I don't know how we can find him," Lucas said sadly. "He could be anywhere. I wish he'd left some sort of sign. Anything to point us in his direction."

Princess Pulverizer's eyes brightened. "I know something that will point us to him!" The princess reached into her bag and pulled out a long arrow.

"How will that help?" Lucas asked.

"Don't you remember?" the princess exclaimed. "It was a gift from the mayor of Ire-Mire-Briar-Shire. He told us, 'If ever the holder of the arrow finds themselves lost, it will always point them toward home.' "

"But we're not lost," Lucas insisted. "Dribble is. Or at least *we* lost *him*. And I don't want to go home until we find him."

"My father told me that home is where your family is," Princess Pulverizer said. "As long as we're on this Quest of Kindness together, Dribble is part of our family. So the arrow will point us to where he is."

"I don't think it works that way," Lucas argued.

"It does," Princess Pulverizer assured him. "How do you think I found you and Dribble that time you were held prisoner in Sir Surly's cottage?" The arrow began twisting toward the left in her hands. "See? We have to go this way. Now hurry!"

◇ ◇ ◇ ◇ ◇

"I think the arrow's broken," Lucas complained some time later. "We've been walking for quite a while. I haven't seen one sign of Dribble."

Princess Pulverizer hated to admit it, but Lucas was right. This time the arrow didn't seem to be of any help. "I know," she said. "Let's take a break and—"

Splash!
Princess
Pulverizer
stepped right
into a giant
puddle. A blast
of purple water
splattered all
around her.

"Those are dragon tears!" Lucas shouted out excitedly. "Dribble's got to be around here somewhere. The arrow is taking us to him. You were right!"

"Of course I was," Princess Pulverizer responded. "I never doubted it for a second."

The sword of truth began to quiver at the princess's side. Okay, so maybe she'd doubted it for a second.

"Here's another puddle," Lucas said as he followed the path of purple puddles. "And another . . . And anoth—"

Bonk! Lucas ran right into Dribble.

"I found him!" Lucas shouted, hugging the big green dragon with joy.

"Hello, little buddy. Hello, Princess," Dribble greeted them sadly. "I was hoping you two wouldn't find me."

"Why would you say that?" Princess Pulverizer asked him. "We're here to clear your name."

"You can't," Dribble told her.

"Of course we can," Princess Pulverizer said. "You'll come back to town and tell everyone you didn't do it. Of course, we'll have to free a unicorn in order to convince them you're telling the truth, but—"

Dribble gave her a funny look. "Free a *unicorn*?"

"It's a long story," Lucas told him. "We'll explain on our way back to Beeten Wheeten."

"I'm not going back to Beeten Wheeten," Dribble said. "And you two will have to finish the Quest of Kindness without me."

"Don't be ridiculous," Princess

Pulverizer said. "You will continue the quest. And soon everyone will know you didn't burn down that barn."

"You don't understand," Dribble told her. "Those people were right. I *did* burn down the barn. *It was all my fault.*"

CHAPTER 8

Princess Pulverizer stood there, waiting for the sword of truth to start wiggling and jiggling at Dribble's obvious lie.

But the sword didn't wave. It hung still at her side. Dribble was telling the truth.

"*You* burned down the barn?" Lucas asked Dribble. "Why?"

"I woke up with a bad stomachache," Dribble recalled. "So I went for a walk, to try and feel better."

"That sometimes works," Lucas agreed. "We've been walking a long time and I feel better now."

"It didn't help me," Dribble said. "I just got gassier. The heartburn was awful."

Princess Pulverizer was trying to be patient, but this story was getting to be too long. "Can you get to the part where you set the barn on fire?" she asked.

"I am," Dribble insisted. "As I walked past the barn, I let out a huge burp. A spark popped out of my mouth and landed on the wooden barn. That's when my heartburn caused *barn* burn." A flood of purple tears started to flow from Dribble's eyes. "So you see, it's all my fault."

"No, it's not," the princess insisted.

"Weren't you listening?" Dribble asked. "I burped the spark that burned the barn."

"Only because someone made you—and pretty much the rest of the village—really sick," Princess Pulverizer said.

"Really?" Dribble asked.

"Yeah," Lucas said. "Nearly everyone in town has a stomachache. And they say they've had them for a while. But it seemed worse today."

"Once we find out what's making everyone sick, we'll find out who is *really* responsible for that fire," Princess Pulverizer said.

"What if no one's responsible?" Dribble asked. "What if it's just a stomach flu?"

Princess Pulverizer thought back to the long line by the public bathroom. "Too many people have been sick for too long for it to just be some sort of flu," she said.

"You aren't sick," Dribble pointed out.

"I have a really strong stomach," Princess Pulverizer boasted.

Lucas gave Dribble a hug. "I'm just glad we proved you're not a barn-burning kind of dragon," he told his pal.

"Oh, we haven't proven anything . . . yet," Princess Pulverizer said.

Dribble and Lucas stared at her.

"I mean, we need to figure out what is getting everyone sick," the princess continued. "And let the people of Beeten Wheeten know. Otherwise, they're still going to think Dribble is guilty."

"How are we going to figure that out?" Lucas asked her.

Princess Pulverizer thought for a moment. "There had to be something you ate or did earlier in the day that gave you bad gas," she said. "We have to go back to

Beeten Wheeten and retrace your steps."

"That's a great idea!" Lucas exclaimed.

"No, it's a terrible idea," Dribble said.

The princess was shocked. "Why?"

"I can't go back there," Dribble said. "Everyone wants to slay me."

"Oh, right," Princess Pulverizer said. "I forgot."

"*I* didn't," Dribble replied sadly.

Princess Pulverizer thought for a while. There had to be some way to sneak Dribble into town. *But how?* It wasn't like a big green dragon could just walk unnoticed into Beeten Wheeten.

Or could he?

Princess Pulverizer raced over to a nearby pine tree. She pulled out her sword and swiftly sliced off a branch that was thick with green needles.

"What are you doing?" Lucas asked her.

"Making a disguise for Dribble," the princess said. "How else are we going to sneak him into Beeten Wheeten?"

"What are you trying to disguise me as?" Dribble asked.

"A tree," Princess Pulverizer replied. She sliced at another branch. "Timber!" she called as the branch fell to the ground.

"You want to sneak me into town as a walking, talking tree?" Dribble asked. "That makes no sense."

"Of course not," the princess said.

"But you just said—" Lucas began.

"Dribble can walk and talk when he's alone with us," Princess Pulverizer explained. She looked up at the dragon. "Once we get to the village, you have to stand really still near the trees on the grass near the edge of the square. And keep your snout shut."

"It could work," Lucas said. "You're already green, Dribble. And you're pretty tall." He gathered a few pinecones to add to the dragon's tree costume.

"Of course it will work," Princess Pulverizer insisted. She used some twine from her knapsack to tie the branches to Dribble's arms and legs.

"Come on, Lucas. Climb up Dribble's tail and put these sticky, sap-covered pine branches on his head."

Dribble frowned as the needles pricked his skin. "These things are itchy," he complained. "This is just ridiculous. No one is going to believe I'm a tree."

Just then a bluebird flew over and landed on Dribble's head. She began pecking at him—and building a nest.

"*There's* someone that believes you're a tree," Princess Pulverizer told the dragon.

"You won't be in the disguise for long," Lucas assured his pal. "Just until we clear your name."

"And hopefully help the sick folks in Beeten Wheeten, too," Princess Pulverizer added. "Dribble, you should hear the moaning, groaning, and burping that's going on there. You have to help us figure this out. If not for yourself, then for the people of Beeten Wheeten."

Dribble let out a big sigh and looked down at his friends. "Well, what are you waiting for?" he asked. "Get moving. You have a lot of pine branches to stick on. And maybe add a pinecone or two on my tail."

CHAPTER 9

"This tree disguise better work," Dribble said as the three friends made their way through the woods toward Beeten Wheeten. "If it doesn't, those people are going to cut me down and slay me."

"It *will* work," said Princess Pulverizer. "You look just like a pine tree."

The sword of truth wiggled at her side.

"If you say so," Dribble replied doubtfully.

"Let's try and figure out what got you sick, Dribble," Lucas said, changing the subject. "What was the first thing you did that morning?"

"I got up, brushed my teeth, and made a grilled cheese sandwich for breakfast."

"Then we went into the woods and you started making sandwiches for your restaurant," Princess Pulverizer continued. "None of those things would make you sick, though."

"P.U." Lucas held his nose shut. "What's that smell?"

Dribble looked around. "I think it's coming from the river. Look at all the garbage floating in there."

"It stinks worse than ever," Lucas said. "Why would anyone dump trash into a river? It's not fair to the fish."

"Or to the folks who drink from the river," Princess Pulverizer added. Suddenly, a lot of things began to make sense. "Dribble, you gulped down a lot of this water the night before the fire. I bet *that's* what made you sick."

"I drank a little," Lucas added. "And my stomach hurt this morning. Princess Pulverizer didn't drink from the river at all. Smart move."

"I guess so," Princess Pulverizer agreed. "I was just lucky they have such wonderful fruit juice in Beeten Wheeten. The only time I was near water is when I brushed my teeth. And I spat that out."

"No wonder I got heartburn!" Dribble exclaimed as he watched a grease-stained dish towel float by.

"All we have to do is figure out who is

dumping this stuff into the river," Princess Pulverizer said. "That's who's really responsible for burning down the barn— and all the tummy trouble."

"How long will *that* take?" Dribble wondered aloud.

"Not long at all. Look!" Princess Pulverizer pointed downstream and frowned. "Why am I not surprised?"

"It's Ralf!" Dribble said.

"That guy is about as rotten as you can get," Lucas added. "He's a litterer, a unicorn capturer, and a lousy juggler."

Princess Pulverizer raised her sword high in the air. "STOP!" she shouted in Ralf's direction.

Ralf looked up. He tossed an old slipper into the river and ran.

"Halt!" she yelled. "I have come to the rescue of the people of Beeten Wheeten!"

"You and what army?" Ralf called back. "That wimpy kid?"

"Who are you calling wimpy?" Dribble asked. Then he remembered he was supposed to be a tree. He shut his mouth.

But it was too late.

"Who said that?" Ralf demanded.

"Um . . . I did," Lucas lied.

"Didn't sound like you," Ralf said.

"Well, it was," Lucas replied.

But Ralf didn't hear Lucas's reply. He had already disappeared into the woods.

"Come on, you two!" Princess Pulverizer exclaimed as she took off after Ralf. "We can't let him get away!"

"Where do you think Ralf is?" Lucas asked a few minutes later as the three friends arrived in Beeten Wheeten's village square.

"I don't know," Princess Pulverizer admitted. "But he can't hide forever. We're going to find him."

"There are a lot of people here," Dribble said. "I'll bet he's hiding in this crowd."

"Shhh . . . ," Lucas warned the dragon. "Someone might hear you."

"Lucas is right," Princess Pulverizer

added. "You have to stand right here and not move. We'll take it from here."

With that, Princess Pulverizer walked to the center of the square and called out, "People of Beeten Wheeten, I know why you are ill! Ralf the juggler has been dumping garbage into your river! He's poisoning your water with trash."

A crowd of people turned toward her. The princess couldn't believe how sick they looked. And boy, were they burping.

"Ralf is the reason you're gassy," she continued. "He's the reason that barn burned down. Dribble the dragon got heartburn and burped a flame. It was an accident. And it was caused by Ralf."

"Don't blame me!" Ralf shouted as he suddenly emerged from the crowd, Bertha by his side. "I have done nothing wrong."

"I saw you dumping trash into the river," the princess proclaimed. "So did Lucas. And so did . . ." She stopped herself midsentence. She didn't want to give Dribble away. "And so did a whole lot of birds and squirrels," she added quickly.

"So what?" Ralf said. "I have a lot of trash. You people throw a lot of junk at me every day. It was smelling up my stage and campsite. I had to get rid of it."

"I drink the water that flows downstream from your campsite," a woman with a particularly sick expression on her face said. "So do my neighbors. There's a lot of trash in our water."

"There would be less if you people didn't throw things at me during my act," Ralf told her angrily. "Anyway, my trash isn't what has caused your problems. It's this girl and her friends who have brought on the worst of your illness."

"That's not true!" the princess insisted.

"Of course it is," Ralf said. "The people were only a little sick until you got here. It's after they ate those greasy grilled cheeses that things got really bad."

The sword of truth began to wiggle. "You're lying!" Princess Pulverizer shouted. "And this sword of truth proves it."

A murmur went through the crowd. Princess Pulverizer smiled. The people were coming around to her side.

"There's no such thing as a sword of truth," Ralf told the crowd. "She's making it up. *She's* the actual liar."

The crowd murmured again.

"People are just getting sicker because the water is getting more polluted every day," Lucas insisted.

"Not true," Ralf said. "It's because of your rotten sandwiches."

"They are *not* rotten!" Lucas argued.

"Why don't we let the unicorn decide who is telling the truth?" Princess Pulverizer suggested. "Ralf, you told me yourself that unicorns can tell if someone is lying. Let the unicorn out of its cage. Let's see who gets poked by his horn."

Lucas nodded. "Great idea!" he said. "It's an easy way to prove the truth. And we don't have to go very far. Your stage—

and the unicorn cage—is just past those houses over there."

"Not gonna happen," Ralf said. "You're trying to trick me. The minute I open that cage, the unicorn is going to run away. I captured him fair and square. And I'm keeping him in the cage."

"You're just afraid that unicorn will show everyone what an evil, moneygrubbing, lying polluter you are," Lucas said angrily.

Whoa! That was pretty strong language coming from Lucas. He didn't sound meek or lily-livered at all.

"I'm not the one the people of Beeten Wheeten should fear," Ralf told Lucas. "It's you and your friends. Ever since . . ."

Ralf droned on and on, but Princess Pulverizer was barely listening. She was too busy scanning the crowd for any signs of a dragon dressed as a tree. During the argument, Dribble had drifted from the spot where she and Lucas had left him.

"I think this girl may be as bad as the dragon himself," Ralf continued. "We need to rid our town of these folks . . ."

"Run free!" a bellowing voice sounded from the far end of the square—just

beyond the houses, near Ralf's stage *and the unicorn cage*.

Princess Pulverizer gasped. She'd know that voice anywhere. It belonged to Dribble. What was that dragon doing? He was sure to give himself away.

The crowd hurried toward the stage. Many arrived just in time to see the unicorn bolting from its open cage.

Princess Pulverizer looked around for Dribble. But all she saw were pine trees.

Then she noticed that one of the trees had eyes. And a snout.

Quickly, Princess Pulverizer hurried over to the dragon's side. "What did you do?" she whispered.

"That lock's not very strong," Dribble whispered back. "At least not for a dragon. I snapped it in half with one claw and set the unicorn free."

"But we needed the unicorn to prove your innocence," Princess Pulverizer said.

"That's not as important as freeing that poor little animal," Dribble said. "You'll figure out another way to clear my name. I have faith in you."

Princess Pulverizer felt very proud that her friend believed in her.

She just wished she knew how to help.

"Which one of you let my unicorn loose?" Ralf angrily asked.

"That's not *your* unicorn," Lucas told Ralf indignantly. "It doesn't belong to you. It shouldn't belong to *anyone*."

"I captured him fair and square," Ralf argued. "And I'm going to get him back!"

"Run, unicorn, run!" Dribble shouted. Then he clamped his snout fast. But it was too late. Everyone had heard him.

"Did that tree just say something?" someone in the crowd asked with surprise.

Ralf looked at Dribble suspiciously. "That's no tree!" he exclaimed, yanking the pine needles right off Dribble's face. "That's a dragon!"

"Ow!" Dribble cried out. "That hurt. This sap is very sticky."

The crowd gasped.

"Here's the creature who burned down that barn," Ralf told the crowd. "I told you these strangers were up to no good."

Dribble began to tremble. Lucas ran to his side.

"Slay the dragon! Slay the dragon!" A loud chant rose up among the crowd.

The unicorn stopped in its tracks. It turned and charged furiously back toward the village square.

"He's coming for the dragon!" Ralf exclaimed. "The unicorn knows he burned that barn down on purpose."

Dribble stood there, frozen, staring at the crowd of people who wanted to slay him, and at the unicorn, who seemed to be charging right at him.

As the unicorn came close, Ralf leaped

out of the way, giving the creature a clear path straight to Dribble.

"You see," Ralf told the people of Beeten Wheeten. "I'm not guilty of anything. The unicorn knows the truth."

Princess Pulverizer gulped. The unicorn *was* headed right for her friend. And he did not seem to be stopping.

CHAPTER 10

"Ow! That horn is sharp!"

The people of Beeten Wheeten gasped as the unicorn made a sudden turn, then jabbed Ralf in the leg with its horn.

"It's Ralf's fault my barn is now a giant ash pile!" the farmer shouted.

"It's Ralf's fault I was puking my guts out all night!" another man added.

"That's not true!" Ralf exclaimed. He turned to face the crowd of people coming up behind him. "The unicorn made a mistake. This proves nothing."

The unicorn lowered his head and butted Ralf right in the rear end.

"It's no mistake," Princess Pulverizer said. She reached over and quickly yanked the copy of *Unicorns from A to Z* from Ralf's back pocket.

"Hey, that's mine!" Ralf shouted.

"OW!" He let out a squeal of pain as the unicorn butted him again.

"It's on page 37," Princess Pulverizer continued. *"Unicorns have the unique ability to spot a liar. If a unicorn senses someone is telling a lie, he will poke him with his horn."* She smiled triumphantly. "You were lying when you said Dribble started the fire on purpose."

"Ouch!" Ralf exclaimed as the unicorn poked him in the rear end once again. "That's it! I'm out of here."

Ralf started running down the road.

"Ralf!" Bertha called as she hurried after him. "Wait for me!"

But Ralf didn't wait. He couldn't. Not with the unicorn following him so closely and poking his rear end.

"I guess I owe you an apology, big

fella," the farmer said as he headed over to Dribble. "We all do."

Purple tears started flowing from Dribble's eyes. Princess Pulverizer was pretty sure they were tears of joy this time.

"It's okay," Dribble said. "For a while even I started to believe I was guilty."

"It was a good thing that unicorn knew who the *real* liar was," Lucas said. "Capturing him sure backfired on Ralf."

"Yes," the farmer agreed. "But now we all have to undo the mess Ralf left. It will take us months to clean out that river."

"We'll help you," Dribble said. "Right, Princess Pulverizer?"

"Huh?" Princess Pulverizer looked up at the sound of her name. She hadn't heard the farmer or Dribble. She'd been too busy reading about unicorns in Ralf's book.

"I said, we can stick around for a while and help these nice people clean up their river," Dribble repeated.

"I don't think that will be necessary," Princess Pulverizer replied.

Dribble stared at her. "I thought you wanted to be a knight. No truly kind knight would leave these people with a river filled with garbage."

"I'm not doing that," the princess assured Dribble. "I'm just saying they won't need our help. It says in this book that a unicorn can purify water with his horn. So all we have to do is get the unicorn to stick his horn in the river, and it will be cleaned up in an instant. Easy peasy."

"That's a great idea!" Lucas exclaimed.

Princess Pulverizer beamed with pride.

"It's not easy," Dribble argued. "Or peasy."

"It's not?" Lucas wondered.

"*Why* not?" the princess demanded.

"Because the unicorn is gone," Dribble reminded them. "And I don't think he's coming back."

"I don't blame him," Lucas said. "He thinks Princess Pulverizer tricked him into being captured."

The crowd stared at them, surprised.

"Why would you do that?" the farmer's wife demanded.

"I didn't," the princess insisted. "At least I didn't mean to. Ralf tricked me."

"But the unicorn doesn't know that," Dribble said.

"I suppose not," Princess Pulverizer agreed. "I wouldn't blame him for never trusting me again."

The princess sighed. She wanted to move on and finish the rest of her good deeds in her Quest of Kindness. But she knew that wasn't possible right then. She had to stay and help the people of Beeten Wheeten clean their river.

It wasn't that cleaning out a polluted river wasn't a good deed. It was just that it was going to take *so long*. And that river smelled awful.

"I guess we should get started," Princess Pulverizer finally said. "Grab some trash bags and clothespins."

"Why clothespins?" Lucas asked.

"For our noses," she replied. "No one wants to smell that trash all day."

◈ ◈ ◈ ◈ ◈

"Dribble, will you please make us some sandwiches as we clean up?" the mayor of Beeten Wheeten asked the dragon. "This work is making us all very hungry."

Dribble smiled widely. "Of course," he said. "It will be my pleasure."

"He looks happy," Lucas told Princess Pulverizer.

"Why wouldn't he be?" she replied, sounding quite grouchy. "He's over there making sandwiches, while we're here wading through Ralf's garbage." She shoved some moldy bread covered in rancid lard into her trash bag and tried not to gag.

"Dribble is helping in his own way," Lucas said.

"I guess," Princess Pulverizer agreed. "It's just—"

"Shhhhh." Lucas shushed her.

"I beg your pardon?" Princess Pulverizer demanded angrily. She was not used to being shushed.

"Listen," Lucas said nervously. "Someone is hiding in the bushes. Do you think it could be Ralf? Maybe he came back for revenge."

"He wouldn't dare," Princess Pulverizer replied.

Or would he?

CHAPTER 11

Ever so slowly, Princess Pulverizer edged toward the nearby bushes. Somebody had to confront Ralf, or whoever was lurking nearby. It might as well be her.

With one swift move of her hand, Princess Pulverizer whipped the branches of the bushes aside. And as she did, she came face-to-face with . . .

The unicorn! He'd come back.

The beautiful white creature stared at Princess Pulverizer.

The princess flashed him her friendliest smile—which apparently wasn't friendly enough. The unicorn dashed away.

"Don't run!" the princess called to him. "I would never hurt you."

But the unicorn raced off, running through the crowd of people. He was headed straight for Dribble.

Princess Pulverizer gulped. What was this about? Had the unicorn finished poking Ralf, and now it was back to accuse Dribble of something?

Everyone stopped cleaning. They turned and watched as the unicorn lowered his head. He took straight aim right at Dribble. And then . . . he gently rubbed his soft white head against the dragon's tough green hide.

"He's thanking you for freeing him!"

Lucas declared with excitement.

Princess Pulverizer let out a sigh. "Well, that's a relief," she said.

"What did you think he was going to do?" Dribble asked her.

"Me?" Princess Pulverizer asked. "Um, nothing. I knew all along he was here to thank you."

The sword of truth jiggled at her side.

"Anyway, now he can help us clean this river," she continued.

"If he wants to," Dribble said. He looked at the people of Beeten Wheeten. "It's not like he owes anyone here a favor. Not one of you came to his rescue. In fact, you paid money to stare at him."

The people of Beeten Wheeten looked at the ground, embarrassed.

The unicorn glanced at the polluted

river. A single rainbow-colored tear fell from his eye. Ever so slowly, he walked toward the water, with his head lowered.

When the unicorn reached the water's edge, he dipped his horn into the river. There was a flash of light. A sweet-smelling wind blew through the trees. And in an instant, the river was clean.

"I guess unicorns don't hold grudges," Lucas said.

"Good thing," Princess Pulverizer agreed.

"It's also a good thing that Dribble freed that unicorn," Lucas told her. "With his help we were able to clear Dribble's name *and* clear the river."

"Speaking of which, we've done our good deed," Princess Pulverizer told the crowd of people who had gathered at the riverbank. "Beeten Wheeten is a healthy place to live again. We should be on our way."

"Before you go, I'd like to give you something," the mayor of Beeten Wheeten told the princess. He reached into his pocket and pulled out a white handkerchief with a colorful unicorn embroidered on it. "This has belonged to my family for a long time. I'd like you to have it as our way of saying thank you."

Princess Pulverizer reached out to take the handkerchief. Then she thought better of it.

"Dribble is the one you should be thanking," she said. "He risked his own safety to free the unicorn."

"You're right," the mayor said. "Dribble, this is for you. Keep it safe. Because this

is a special, magical handkerchief. Hold it
to your nose, and you will be able to smell
things miles away."

Princess Pulverizer laughed. "I guess
we're lucky this river smells better now."

"No kidding," Dribble agreed. He held the handkerchief up to his snout. "I smell lemons. And there are no lemon trees around."

"I didn't even see a lemonade *stand* in Beeten Wheeten," Princess Pulverizer added. "Lots of fruit juice stands. But no lemonade."

"The next lemonade stand is three towns over," the mayor told them.

"Wow!" Dribble exclaimed. "This thing really works."

"I hope that handkerchief is as helpful to you as you've been to us," the mayor told him sincerely.

The unicorn began nudging Dribble gently with his head.

"I think he wants to go home," Dribble said.

"It's time for us all to be going," Princess Pulverizer added.

"Come back anytime," the mayor of Beeten Wheeten told Princess Pulverizer and her pals. "And bring some of Dribble's grilled cheese sandwiches!"

"Let's walk him home," Dribble said. "I want to make sure he gets there safely."

Princess Pulverizer agreed. She couldn't wait to see a whole herd of unicorns.

"I wonder if the unicorn has a name," Lucas said.

"I'd like to call him Fortune," Dribble said. "Because it was my good fortune that he came along to save me."

"We would have rescued you," Princess Pulverizer insisted. "Eventually."

"Maybe," Dribble agreed. "But *he's* the one who did."

"Do you like the name Fortune?" Lucas asked the unicorn.

The gentle creature swished his tail happily.

"That settles it," Dribble said. "You're Fortune."

The group walked on for a while, following Fortune home. They strode past blossoming trees, thick green bushes, and some shimmery orange, yellow, and gold flowers Princess Pulverizer had never seen before. This was clearly no ordinary part of the forest.

Fortune slowed and stopped in a clearing. He looked around and let out a delicate call that sounded a great deal like a turtledove's cry.

No one answered.

That's because there was no one around *to* answer. The clearing was empty. There wasn't a unicorn in sight.

The only thing left to prove they'd ever been there were faint hoofprints in the grass.

"Something's happened," Lucas said.

"Something *awful*, I fear," Princess Pulverizer added.

Fortune bowed his head. A rainbow tear rolled down his cheek.

"We have to help Fortune find his herd." Dribble petted the unicorn gently on his head.

"I agree," Lucas said. "But how do we do that? The hoofprints are heading in different directions. Do you have any ideas, Princess Pulverizer?"

"Not yet," she admitted. "But I know we've already found something *very* important."

"What's that?" Dribble asked.

"The next good deed on our Quest of Kindness," the princess answered. "We're going to help Fortune find his family."

Dribble nodded in agreement. "That could be our most important good deed yet!"

Princess PULVERIZER

Collect each adventure on your reading quest!

Nancy Krulik

is the author of more than two hundred books for children and young adults, including three *New York Times* Best Sellers.

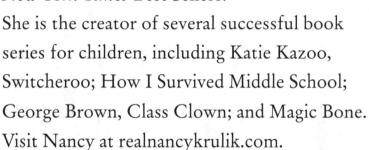

She is the creator of several successful book series for children, including Katie Kazoo, Switcheroo; How I Survived Middle School; George Brown, Class Clown; and Magic Bone. Visit Nancy at realnancykrulik.com.

Justin Rodrigues

is a character designer and visual development artist based in Los Angeles, California. He has worked for acclaimed studios including DreamWorks Animation, Disney Television Animation, Marvel, Fisher-Price, and many more.